To our lovely newest princesses, Kyla and Lily
—F.P.H.

To F.P.H., whose work always inspires
—L.S.

Text copyright © 2009 by Florence Parry Heide
Illustrations copyright © 2009 by Lane Smith

Published in the United States
by Schwartz & Wade Books,
an imprint of Random House Children's Books,
a division of Random House, Inc.,
New York.

Schwartz & Wade Books and the colophon are trademarks of Random House, Inc.

Visit us on the Web! www.randomhouse.com/kids

Educators and librarians, for a variety of teaching tools, visit us at www.randomhouse.com/teachers

Library of Congress Cataloging-in-Publication Data
Heide, Florence Parry.
Princess Hyacinth: the suprising tale of a girl who floated / Florence Parry Heide ; illustrated by Lane Smith. – 1st ed.
p. cm.
Summary: Princess Hyacinth is bored and unhappy sitting in her palace every day because,
unless she is weighed down by specially-made clothes, she will float away,
but her days are made brighter when kite-flying Boy stops to say hello.
ISBN 978-0-375-84501-7 (hardcover)–ISBN 978-0-375-93753-8 (Gibraltar lib. bdg.)
[1. Princesses–Fiction. 2. Floating bodies–Fiction.] I. Smith, Lane, ill. II. Title.
PZ7.H36St 2009
[E]–dc22
2008039923

The text of this book is set in Garamond Premier Pro.
The characters in this book were created in brush and ink on watercolor paper;
the backgrounds were painted in oil on board and then combined on a Macintosh computer.
Book design by Molly Leach

MANUFACTURED IN CHINA

10 9 8 7 6 5 4 3 2 1

First Edition

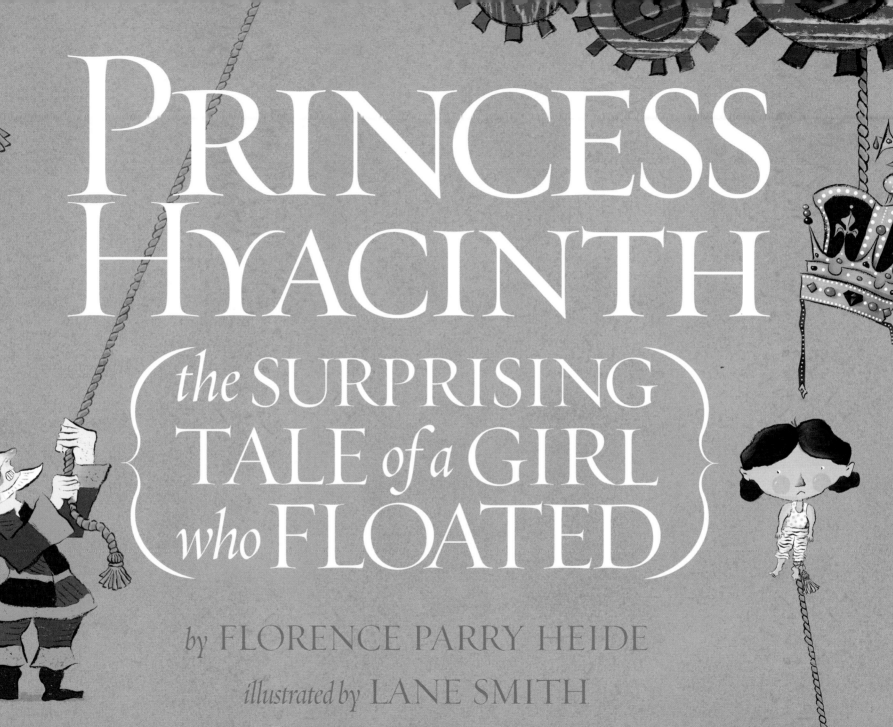

PRINCESS HYACINTH
(the SURPRISING TALE of a GIRL who FLOATED)

by FLORENCE PARRY HEIDE

illustrated by LANE SMITH

DESIGN BY MOLLY LEACH

schwartz & wade books   new york

Princess Hyacinth had a problem.

Well, you're saying, everyone has a problem.
But this was an *unusual* problem. Oh, she didn't
look unusual, *that* wasn't it. She had two eyes, with
a nose between them and a mouth under that—you
know, the usual things in the usual arrangement.

In fact, if she wasn't all dressed
up in her Princess clothes, you'd
think she was just anybody.

So what was the problem?

Princess Hyacinth floated.

Unless she was attached to something, or weighted down, she just floated— *up, up, up.*

So the King and Queen had little golden weights sewn into the hems of Princess Hyacinth's gowns, and little diamond pebbles sewn into the tops of her socks. Her crown had the heaviest jewels of the kingdom, and a rhinestone strap under her chin to keep it on.

As long as she was all dressed up in her Princess things, she didn't float at all. In fact, she could hardly *move*. But the minute her crown was off, and her gown, and all that . . .

up, up, up she would go in her Royal Underwear.

The only time she could take off her royal stuff was when she was in the palace. *Then* if she floated—and of course she did—she'd just float up to the ceiling and they could always get her down in the morning.

"Why can't I float around outside?" was a question Princess Hyacinth had asked six million times.

"Because you'd just float away altogether," her parents explained.

Poor Princess Hyacinth!

She wished she could run outside, like the children who came to play on the Palace Grounds.

Instead, she sat at the window in her Royal Bathing Suit wearing a seat belt, looking at all the children having fun.

One was a redheaded boy who could fly his sky-blue kite higher than all the others. His name was Boy. He waved at Princess Hyacinth every day, and she waved back. He smiled at her, and she smiled back. Boy had painted a gold crown on his kite in honor of the Princess.

Wasn't that nice?

Boy had come over to her window to say hello a couple of times. Well, *seven* times— she had counted every single one.

Today he walked over again.
"I like your kite," said Princess Hyacinth.
"I like your crown," said Boy.

He turned to go.

"And I like *you*," he said over his shoulder.

At least, that's what Princess Hyacinth *thought* he said.

Maybe he had just said "Toodle-oo."
Or "Yike-a-doodle-doo."
She couldn't be sure.

After a while the children left the Palace Grounds.

"I'm terribly, horribly, dreadfully bored," said the Princess.
She decided to go to the park.

Of course, she had to get all dressed up in her Princess clothes first.

The weights and everything.
The crown and everything.

And then off she went,
walking to the park.

Well, she wasn't exactly
walking, she was sort
of dragging along.

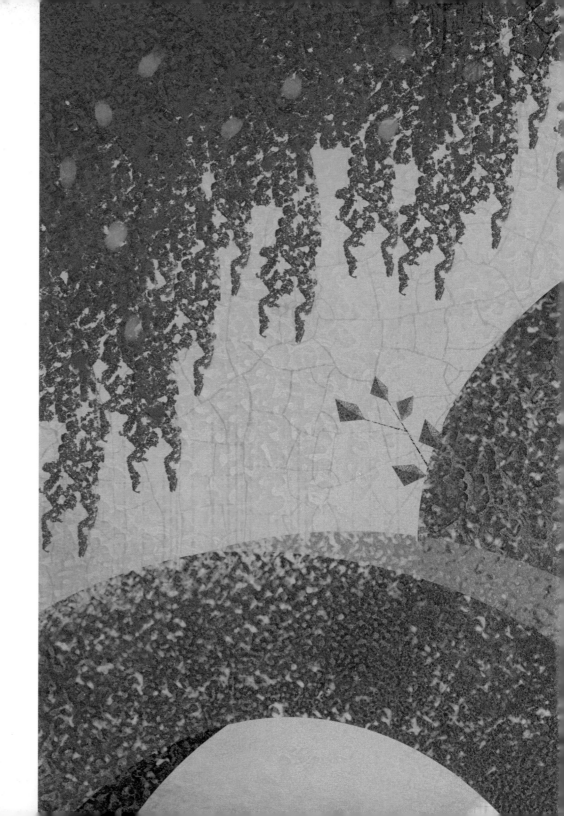

She saw a balloon man coming toward her.
Suddenly Princess Hyacinth had an exciting idea!

"Mr. Balloon Man," she said,
"I'd like to float up there with the balloons."
"That," said the Balloon Man, "is impossible."

"No it isn't," said Princess Hyacinth firmly.
"If I took off all my Princess clothes, you could
tie a string to my ankle and I could float."

"Oh, dear," said the Balloon Man.
But since she was the Princess, she got her way.

Princess Hyacinth took off everything from tip to toe (except her Royal Underwear) and put it in a neat pile under her umbrella.

She left a sign:

Do not touch! Property of the Princess

The Balloon Man tied a string to her ankle and held on to the other end, and up she went. "I feel like a balloon!" said the Princess.

The Balloon Man walked through the park, and Princess Hyacinth bobbed along with the balloons.

It was pretty exciting.

But alas and alack!

Somehow or other the Balloon Man
let go of the string that was attached
to Princess Hyacinth.

And *up* she went.

"Oh, wow," said the Princess.

The Balloon Man ran to tell a policeman.
The policeman told the Palace Guards.
The Palace Guards notified the King and Queen.

"Oh, dear," said the Queen.

The King got out his binoculars so that he
could watch the Princess as she floated *up and up*.
"As long as I keep an eye on her,
she won't get into any trouble," he said.

Princess Hyacinth floated higher and higher.
But hey! She loved this free-bird feeling!

She **whirled** and she **twirled**,

she **swooshed**
and she **swirled**,

she **zigged** and she
zagged and she
zigzagged.

She **zoomed** and **caroomed** and **cartwheeled**.

She did handsprings and headstands,

flip-flops and fandangos.

It was the most fun
she had ever had
in her whole life.

And all the time, she was floating *up, up, up.*
Now she couldn't even see the castle.

I never knew the sky was so high, she thought.

She saw something nearby.
What could it be?

She looked closer.
What was it?

It was her crown!
Her golden crown!
What was it doing here?
She was close enough
now to touch it.

Look! It was Boy's
kite with the painting
of her crown!

Oh, my.
Before she knew it,
she was tangled up.

Now what?

Down on the ground,
Boy felt a tug and
started to reel in his kite.

Princess and all.

The King, who had been watching her
through his binoculars (so that she wouldn't
get into any trouble), saw the whole thing.

Oh, hooray!

Princess Hyacinth had been rescued!

Boy was a hero.
The King gave him a bag of gold.

Now what?

Well, since Princess Hyacinth had had such a wonderful time floating up there in the air, she wanted to do that every single day.

And she did.

Every day she went out to the Palace
Grounds in her Royal Underwear, and *up, up, up*
she would float.

Then Boy would fly his kite *up, up, up*
right next to her, and reel her
in when she wanted to come down.

And then she would invite him into the palace for tea and popcorn.

The problem about the floating was never solved, and that's too bad.

But Princess Hyacinth was never bored again.

Good.

DATE DUE

JAN 1 9	SEP 23		
FEB 1 8	MAR 21		
MAR 8			
DEC 8			
JAN 2 0			
MAR 6			
DEC 1 7			
MAY 2 9			
OCT 3 1			
JAN 2 1			
FEB 17			
MAR 1 7			
MAR 2 6			
APR 9			
NOV 9			
MAY 1 2			